Northern Narratives #4

TALL TALES OF ALASKA

SKAGWAY AK

Gateway to the
Klondike Gold Rush

W.R. Kozey

ISBN 978-1-954896-49-9 paperback
ISBN 978-1-954896-48-2 ebook
Printed in United States

Illustrations and cover design: Sam Grubitz

Cover image: National Park Service, Klondike Gold Rush National Historical Park, George and Edna Rapuzzi Collection, KLGO 55832a.
Gift of the Rasmuson Foundation.

Southeast Alaska map iStock.com/Artist Rainer Lesniewski.

Fathom Publishing Company
PO Box 200448 | Anchorage, AK 99520
Fathom Publishing.com

To my father,
who showed me that hard work
is its own kind of magic.
May this book honor your life and
all the sacrifices you made for me.

Contents

Acknowledgments

I would like to begin by acknowledging the Indigenous peoples of Alaska and their ancestral homelands. I want to pay my respects to all the Tribes that call this land their home and recognize the deep and abiding connections they have to this place.

I would also like to acknowledge the brave and tenacious souls who traveled to Alaska seeking fortune and adventure.
For it is their experiences and struggles that line these pages and without them there is no book.

Finally, I want to express my gratitude to all those who have contributed to this work, whether through guidance, support, or inspiration. This collection would not have been possible without their contributions— thank you.

What came first,
the Skagway or the Dyea?

For many, the lure of Alaska begins with the gold rush—the fever, the fortune, and the sheer madness of it all. Now, you may already know that Skagway was the last stop before the Yukon, the place where stampeders took their final breath before plunging into the unknown. But what you may not know is that Skagway was a sister town. Just across the water, at the mouth of the Taiya River, was Dyea, a town that, for a brief moment, stood as Skagway's equal. Some might even say it came first. And after hearing this story, you may just agree with them.

Now to unravel this mystery, we need to go back, long before the stampeders stormed north, before Skagway got its name, to a time when the Tlingit people used this land as a gathering ground and a hub for trade, treaties, and storytelling with the Indigenous people of the Interior. And all of this was made possible by three defining features of Dyea—the Lynn Canal, the Taiya River, and the legendary Chilkoot Pass.

I say legendary here because the Pass, as you'll learn later in these tales, was the original artery connecting Alaska's coast to the Yukon; and beyond that, the Klondike goldfields. And for the first few thousand prospectors that poured into the area dreaming of gold in their pockets, this was the gateway.

But Dyea had a problem. The Taiya riverbed rose too quickly for ships to dock, which forced the frontiersmen to

wade through ice waters just to reach
land. And unless someone was willing to
build a dock a mile long, the journey to
the Chilkoot started out just that much
chillier. Meanwhile, just around the corner,
the area where Skagway now stands had
something Dyea didn't—deep water.

It wasn't much at first, simply a
convenient landing spot for ships, but
during the gold rush, convenience was
everything. The stampeders were already
carrying backbreaking loads, so they
weren't about to volunteer to haul lumber
to Dyea just to build a pier, which meant
the building supplies stayed in Skagway.

And where there was lumber, there
were real structures—sturdy homes, proper
storefronts, and businesses that didn't
fall over at the first sign of a strong wind.
Dyea, on the other hand, remained rough
and temporary, built only from canvas
and optimism. So, as the gold rush began,
it became a tale of two cities: Dyea, with
its established trail over the mountains,

and Skagway with its docks and deep-water access. That is, until Skagway took a gamble and built its own route to riches—the White Pass Trail. And unlike the brutal Chilkoot Trail, the White Pass allowed prospectors to use pack animals, promising an easier path to the Yukon.

The final blow to the Chilkoot Trail came on Palm Sunday, April 3, 1898. Just outside of Dyea, in the foothills of the Chilkoot, an avalanche crashed into the trail burying over 65 stampeders under a mountain of snow and ice. It was one of the deadliest disasters of the gold rush. And in an instant, for the stampeders already debating which route to take, well, that decision was all but made for them.

More and more, the gold-seekers from down south turned to Skagway. And Skagway grew, leaving Dyea to slowly fade into the history books.

Dyea is all but gone now. But if you ever find yourself in Skagway, and you're looking for something to do that's off the beaten path, take the Dyea Road around Smuggler's Cove. At the end, you won't find the town, but you will find Slide Cemetery where the Palm Sunday victims rest. You'll see the Dyea Campground, where the Taiya River still runs past the empty land where Dyea once stood. And of course, you'll find the trailhead to the famous Chilkoot Pass, where thousands of hopeful miners took their first steps toward their fortune.

So, which came first? Dyea had the trail, the history, and the first rush of treasure hunters. But Skagway had the docks, the infrastructure, and the will to adapt. One town sparked the gold rush. The other survived it. And despite Dyea fading into the trees, its role in history is cemented. For without both of these towns—each with their own role and their own fate—you might never have considered traveling this far north, nor would you be reading this story.

Where did the name Skagway come from?

If you want to understand Skagway's origins, you need to start your search on Fifth Street. There, weathered by the unyielding northern winds, stands a stubborn little log cabin. And according to the plaque, it was built in 1887 by Captain William Moore, which means it predates the gold rush by about a decade.

Captain Moore wasn't just a surveyor, he was also a gambler. And when he looked out over the rugged, windswept valley where Skagway now resides, he made a bold wager. He bet that this place would one day flourish and become a vital port for the state of Alaska. So, he got to work.

The cabin was just the beginning. He milled lumber for docks and buildings, which he used to shape the skeleton of a town that didn't yet exist. Even some of the most famous saloons in town owe their bones to Moore's saw. And while he was at it, he staked a 160-acre claim to the valley itself, calling it Mooresville.

But it wouldn't stay Mooresville for long. No. History would trump ol' Bill's ambition and etch another name into this place. One as unique and unrelenting as the land itself—Skagway.

Where exactly the name came from, no one can say for sure. Most agree that it comes from a Tlingit word which roughly translates to "rugged place, cold place, home to the north wind, home to the whitecaps." And considering the relentless gusts that have battered this valley for centuries, I'd say it's a pretty apt description, don't you?

But a name like that doesn't just come from geography. It comes from a story. And among the locals, there's one legend that lingers still.

Long ago, before Moore arrived, before the stampeders, even before the Russians crossed the Bering Strait, the people of this land told the tale of Skagway, meaning The Beautiful One.

She appeared in the valley as if from nowhere. No family. No past. But the people of the valley took her in, offering food, shelter, and a place among them. She was still an outsider, sure, but they made her feel at home. And after a while she did. But one problem still remained. She didn't have a name. So, the village decided to give her one—Skagway.

And over time, she grew into it. She was striking, strong, and sharp-witted. Her beauty was matched only by her intelligence, and soon she caught the attention of the village chief, who asked her to be his wife. And for a while, they were happy.

That is, until they weren't. On one fateful day, after returning home from an unsuccessful hunt, the chief's frustration boiled over. He yelled at her. He insulted her. He struck her. And whatever love that had once existed between them was shattered.

Skagway, being as independent as she was, walked out. She left the village walking north, climbing higher and higher into the mountains until she was gone. Then came the winds.

Terrible winds tore through the valley with unrelenting force, driving the people to their knees. In their fear, they cried out, "Oh, Skagway! Have mercy on us!" Because they knew. They knew it was her. Her spirit had risen with the mountains, and the winds were her vengeance—a reminder of the cost of cruelty.

Today, her tale endures in Skagway, carried on the gusts that still rake through this valley. So, be kind to your partners. Because you never know when they might rise up and return. Not as a lover, nor as a friend, but as a spiteful wind spirit so strong that they shape the very world around you.

And next time you're in Skagway, if you listen closely through the howl of the north wind, you might just hear her name.

If it's called Skagway, where is Liarsville?

Whether you've visited or are planning to visit Southeast Alaska, the odds are you won't have heard of Liarsville. It doesn't show up on most maps, and it doesn't appear on most people's itinerary. But in the days of the gold rush, it played a critical role in shaping Alaska's biggest boom. It encouraged—or more accurately, convinced—stampeders to travel north straight to Skagway.

But Skagway wasn't the final destination. From here, there was still 600 miles of treacherous terrain separating them from the Klondike goldfields. And for those following along with the *Northern Narrative Series*, you already know that there were easier ways to chase gold.

For instance, Juneau, just 90 miles south of Skagway, was in the middle of a gold boom of its own. It had a saltwater dock, meaning miners could step off a boat and immediately start digging. And even further north, Nome had gold right in the sand, just waiting to be scooped up off of the beach. No passes. No rapids. And no heavy loads to carry.

So, how did Skagway convince thousands of men to take the most brutal, back-breaking route of all to the riches? Its simple, they lied. And that's where Liarsville came in.

Today, Liarsville is a tourist attraction, an open-air museum where visitors can eat salmon, pan for gold, and watch reenactments of the tall tales that shaped the gold rush. But in the late 1800s, the area was much more, and the stories told weren't just for show, they were passed off as fact.

Liarsville is north of Skagway and was home to the journalists covering the gold rush. But something you need to know about these writers is that they weren't your hard-nosed investigative types. They needed Skagway to succeed to keep their jobs and those paychecks coming. So, they sold a fantasy.

They wrote about easy riches and a simple journey north, leaving out the true realities that awaited anyone who took the bait. They didn't mention the Canadian government's one-ton supply rule, which you'll learn about in the following stories. They neglected to describe the boats that had to be built by hand at Lake Bennett which we'll also talk about later. But instead, they spun tales of a golden road paved in opportunity.

And it worked. The stampeders came

in droves. They sold everything, packed up their lives onto their backs, and boarded ships bound for a future that was far hasher than they'd ever imagined.

Skagway thrived because of these stories. It became a booming hub, teeming with fortune-seekers, con men, and opportunists. Back then, it was a rough-and-tumble town where fact and fiction blurred together, and for every hopeful miner, there was someone ready to take advantage of them.

Today, Skagway is a different place. It's a frontier town frozen in time, where wooden boardwalks and gold rush lore attract visitors from all around the world. But somewhere between the past and the present, the real Skagway still exists—a place built on bold dreams and even bigger lies.

So, if you find yourself in town, take it all in. Stroll the streets where stampeders once journeyed toward an uncertain future. Relive the golden dreams that once filled the air. But keep in mind, don't believe everything you hear because stories have a way of stretching the truth—and in Skagway, not everything is exactly as it seems.

Is the golden staircase
made of actual gold?

Since you've been following along,
you know that long before the stampeders
came flooding north, there was only
one way over the coastal mountains
of Southeast Alaska and that was the
Chilkoot Trail. And the trail was used
quite frequently by the Tlingit and other
Indigenous Tribes as a vital trade route
with those living in the Interior. But
when all those prospectors did finally
come, well, this route received a new
pseudonym, one that sounded grand

and divine, like the first steps toward prosperity. They called it the Golden Staircase.

And at first glance, I think we can all agree the name is appealing, a staircase made of fortune and promise. But, of course, the reality was something else entirely. The Staircase wasn't just a climb. It was an ordeal. A brutal, grinding test that offered its own special breed of difficulty. It was the ultimate barrier separating those who had the strength to keep going from those who would turn back, broken and empty-handed.

It didn't just start at the Staircase, though. From the start, the trail did its best to break folks down. It cut through dense forest, crossed frozen rivers, and wound its way through valleys of deep, punishing snow. But that's not what gave it its name. No. After all of that, came the climb.

Out of seemingly nowhere, the trail rises nearly 1,000 feet in less than half a mile—a near-vertical ascent of ice and stone, hacked out with pickaxes, shovels, and sheer determination. By day, the line of men stretched up the mountain like a living chain, each hauling their burden, their breath curling into the cold. By night, in the flickering glow of lanterns, the shadows of weary men filled the gap left by the midnight sun.

Now, if this wasn't bad enough, at the top of the pass stood the Canadian Mounties, enforcing a rule that turned an already punishing journey into something nearly impossible. No one was permitted to cross the border without a year's worth of provisions—an amount that equates to roughly one ton of supplies per person. This burden was far too heavy for a single trip. And so, the Staircase became a relentless cycle. One that went up and down, up and down, for weeks on end.

The stories that came back from this place were haunting. Men spoke of the strange silence on the Staircase—how the vastness of the mountains swallowed

the sound of their struggles. Some told
of the frozen remains left behind at the
summit—half-buried boots, abandoned
sleds, a shovel stuck upright in the snow.
They were all relics of those who climbed
with too much hope and not enough luck.

For some, the trail was too much.
They turned back, leaving their gold-rush
dreams behind to thaw in the spring. For
others, it became a kind of baptism, a
rite of passage that transformed them—
not into prospectors—but hardened
inhabitants of the last frontier.

Now, over time, the Golden Staircase
has become a ghost of its former self; its
glory days remembered only through
the images that line Skagway's postcards,
history books, and museums. But its scars
still remain, chipped directly into the
mountain's face.

Today, the path still remains, co-
managed by Parks Canada and the US
National Park Service. And each summer,
roughly 2,000 hikers retrace it—not for

gold, but for history. They walk the same steps. They breathe the same cold air. And for a moment, they get a glimpse of the price paid by those who came north all those years ago in the pursuit of riches.

Where did the
Deadhorse Trail get its name?

Okay, so now we've established
that one of the routes prospectors took to
the Klondike was the Chilkoot Trail—a
name that, at first glance, almost sounds
inviting. But names can lie. And as we
learned in the last tale, this trail wasn't
a gilded path to riches, but instead, a
crucible carved in ice.

This is why a new route was
established—the White Pass. A broad,
winding trail they were told; a gentler
alternative to the brutal vertical climb of

the Chilkoot Pass. Of course, these were lies as well. And, after the first stampeders traversed the Coast Mountains in the winter time, no one was calling it the White Pass. It had a new name, the Dead Horse Trail.

From the start, the White Pass betrayed its promise. The trail cut through rough terrain—cliffs, ravines, and miles of sucking mud that swallowed boots and hooves alike. But of course, these prospectors didn't know any of this at the time, so the horses, bought fresh off of the ships in Skagway, were loaded beyond their limits, carrying not just the supplies of the men feverish with dreams of gold, but also the weight of desperation.

These men, most of whom were novices and had never saddled a horse in their lives, found themselves betting their fortunes on animals they didn't know how to ride. Unfortunately, many of those horses never stood a chance.

But it wasn't just the terrain that earned the White Pass its grim nickname.

No. It was something much colder than that. The trail, which was promised to be broad enough for wagons, was anything but. It was a narrow, twisting path with drops as far as 400 feet. At first, only a few animals fell, but as the trail climbed higher, the footing grew worse, and the losses came by the dozen. Hooves slipped, packs leaned, and the falls were inevitable.

And no one stopped. If a horse collapsed or fell, the supplies were stripped and maybe the tack was salvaged. The bodies piled up, each horse becoming just another trail marker along the way. Some even said that you could smell the trail long before you saw it. But no one turned back, not for that. The men, still dreaming of the gold and the riches to come, allowed their greed to drown out the carnage around them. And trudge forward they did, their feet sinking in the mud, avoiding the remains of the beasts that had accompanied them this far.

And from what I've been told, by
the time the gold rush peaked, over 3,000
horses had perished on the White Pass.
An example, albeit a brutal one, of the
steep price of chasing fortune in the wilds
of Alaska.

Eventually, though, the White Pass
was tamed—or at least, in a way. And
in 1898, the White Pass Yukon Route
Railroad arrived, carving steel through
the mountains, and negating the use of
the original trail. As for the bones, the
fragments of tack and gear, and the ghostly
remains of the stampeder's ambitions,
those nature took back, as it always does.

But the stories are still told.
Even today, the Dead Horse Trail is
remembered not just as a path to the
Klondike, but as something else—a lesson
of the North. A lesson about ambition,
about greed, and about those who
thought they could cheat the last frontier,
but instead, were swallowed by it.

What is a coffin boat?

In the previous stories, you've heard about the brutal journey north, the competing towns clawing for control, and the bone-crushing slog over both the Chilkoot and White Pass Trails. You know about the stampeders hauling a literal ton of goods, step by agonizing step, thirty times over the mountains. And if you do the math, you'll find that some of these people walked two thousand miles just to cross a fifty-mile trail. Surely, after all that, their troubles were over, right?

Not even close.

Reaching the Yukon side of the mountains didn't mark the end of these prospectors' suffering. It was just the start of a new kind. On the far side of the pass lay Lake Bennett, the first in a long chain of waterways stretching 500 miles to the Klondike goldfields.

Now, in theory, it was simple—follow the river, ride the current, and claim your fortune. But there was one small problem, nobody had told these stampeders that they'd have to build their own boats.

That's right. After surviving one of the hardest overland treks of their lives, would-be-miners were handed a saw, pointed to the trees, and left to figure out how to turn standing timber into something that wouldn't sink along the way. No prior experience. No instructions. No help. Just desperation, brute force, and the blind hope that their hastily made contraption wouldn't send them straight to the bottom of the lake.

Have you ever built a boat?

Me neither. And neither had most of them.

Lake Bennett became a madhouse. Thousands of greenhorn carpenters descended on the Yukon wilderness and turned the shoreline into a sawdust-choked, curse-slinging chaos. Towering pines fell in every direction. And makeshift vessels took shape—some sturdy enough to survive the journey and others looking like they'd be better suited for firewood.

Then came the waiting. As summer faded and the lake froze solid, those who weren't fast enough were then trapped and forced to huddle over fires for the seven, bone-chilling months that is a Yukon winter.

But when the ice finally broke, so too did the tension. And at the peak of the rush, 4,000 boats hit the water all at once. Imagine an overcrowded parking lot, except instead of wagons and carts, it was a floating mass of slapped-together rafts, skiffs, and patched up canoes, all jostling for space on the water. Locals used to say that you could walk from one side of the lake to the other without getting wet just by stepping from boat to boat.

And then came the real danger.

Beyond the lake, the Yukon River turns deadly quick, twisting into two sets of Class V rapids—the highest level of rapid most people can reasonably survive. Some did, but many didn't. And the boats that were smashed to splinters or swallowed whole earned these vessels their unshakable nickname, Coffin Boats.

Some sank outright. Others capsized, taking their cargo—and their crew—with them. But for those who made it through, the river eventually flattened out, the waters grew calm, and on the horizon waited Dawson City, where the possibility of finding gold was still all too real.

The Coffin Boats of the Klondike, as fragile and fleeting as they were, were more than just a desperate means of travel. They were proof of what the stampeders were made of—equal parts determination and delusion.

And to many of them, their journey wasn't about finding gold. It was a test of their grit, ingenuity, and sheer stubborn willpower—a test that featured a hammer, a few planks of pine, and a prayer.

What was Skagway like during the gold rush?

Alright, so you've already read about the journalists—the ones who wrote glowing reports about Skagway, promising wealth and prosperity spilling right out of the ground. And their words convinced plenty of people to sell everything, leave it all behind, and head north to chase gold and glory.

But of course, we know better now. We know about the brutal journey north, the White Pass Trail swallowing man and horse alike, and the Class V rapids waiting on the other side. Clearly, getting to the Klondike goldfields wasn't just hard, it was hell. But what about Skagway itself? That's right, before any of what I just described, stampeders had to make it through town with their goods and their lives.

This was easier said than done. For every miner who made the trek, at least one turned back. And many turned back here. Because Skagway, in those days, was a boomtown, and like many other boomtowns, it was lawless and chaotic. And at the center of it all was one man, Jefferson Randolph Smith, otherwise known as Soapy.

Soapy Smith was, to put it bluntly, a con artist. A snake-oil salesman with a slippery charm, silver tongue, and a talent for deception. And he ran every scam worth running in town, but one of his more notable schemes was his telegraph office.

After the long trip to Skagway, many newcomers wanted to send word home, letting their loved ones know that they were still alive and in one piece. So, they did what anyone would do, they found a telegraph office, paid the clerk a fee, and sent their message—or so they thought.

The year was 1898 and telegraph lines wouldn't reach Skagway until 1901. Meaning, Soapy's wires ran just a few hundred yards into the woods before vanishing in the trees. This was just one of his many tricks.

At his peak, Soapy had over 300 men on his payroll, known as The Soap Gang. And with so many hands on deck to do his dirty work, he was able to paint himself as a respectable town leader—a community benefactor if you will. He claimed to protect Skagway from criminals; criminals who, coincidentally, were his competition. He also donated to charity and even organized the Fourth of July parade in 1898, marching through town like an upstanding citizen.

But his goodwill act only went so far. Just four days after he grand marshaled his parade, the town's law-abiding citizens decided they'd had enough. Soapy's demise occurred down by the docks in an exchange of gunfire with a man named Frank Reid. And when the smoke settled, both men were fatally injured.

Word of the shoot-out spread fast, but it didn't solve Skagway's biggest problem. It was still an unhinged place. And due to its proximity to Canada, the Canadian Northwest Mounted Police had a vested interest. So, they sent a Mountie to take stock of the town and the type of people who were heading toward the Klondike Gold Fields.

The Mountie's name isn't important to this story, but what he said about Skagway is. And from what I've been told, he thought that it was little better than a hell on earth. He also wrote that, at night, the crash of dancehall music would mix with the crackle of gunfire, the cries of murder, and the desperate shouts for help. And in closing, he called Skagway the roughest place he'd ever seen.

So, yes. Before, and even after Soapy was gone, Skagway was a con man's playground. Gangs ran the streets, controlled the law, and turned every unsuspecting miner into a mark. But time has a way of shifting the tide.

And although remnants of Soapy's empire still survive today, instead of criminals and chaos, you'll find one of the best-preserved frontier towns in Alaska. The wooden boardwalks, the false-front buildings, the old saloons—they've all stood the test of time and hold onto a century's worth of stories.

But if you do decide to visit, just make sure to keep an eye on your wallet. Old habits die hard. And you never know when Soapy's ghost might be watching.

How did Soapy Smith
get his name?

Okay, so in the previous story we heard about the early days of Skagway and of Jefferson Randolph Smith, the town's self-proclaimed benefactor. But when Jefferson arrived in Skagway in the late 1890s, his name had already been soaked in infamy. In the newspapers, he'd been called a bunco artist, a confidence man, and a grifter with a smile that could strip the gold fillings from a man's mouth. But to the people who knew him best, he was Soapy. But how did he get such a slick nickname?

Yes, to be a successful con man, to some degree you need to be slippery. But that's not why they called him that. No. He received this nickname more for what he did rather than the type of person he was. And to learn more about the con that got him this moniker, we need to travel—not north to Skagway—but south to Denver, Colorado, where he first learned how easy it was to sell a promise wrapped in paper.

The scam was simple. Smith would position a crate of ordinary soap, stacked high on a street corner. There was nothing special about this soap, the same kind anyone might buy for a few cents at the store. But ol' Soapy never sold anything for what it was worth. In fact, in this instance, he wasn't even selling soap at all—he was selling the idea that it could be worth more.

Here's how it worked, before anyone showed up, he would unwrap a few bars, slip money inside—sometimes one-dollar bills, sometimes a hundred, but always enough to turn heads—and then rewrap them and place them back in the pile. Then, before the crowd, he would auction off the bars, a dollar apiece, maybe two if the crowd seemed eager enough.

Inevitably, someone in the audience would peel back the paper and find a prize. That person, triumphant, would wave their winnings in the air laughing at their luck. The crowd—never content to let another person's fortune pass them by—would press forward, hungry for their own. What they didn't know, though, was that the winner had been planted there from the start. And the rest of the bars held nothing but soap.

And by the time the last bar was sold, Soapy was moving on with pockets full and another area of town in his sights. The trick was old before he got his grip on it, but he played it better than anyone, leaving behind nothing but clean hands and empty wallets.

When the law finally caught on to him in Denver, he moved where the law didn't matter. First, to Creede, Colorado, where the silver flowed faster than the ink on arrest warrants. Then Skagway, where gold fever had turned common sense into a rare commodity. But the name always followed him, outlasting every sheriff, every bounty, and every mark who swore they'd get their money back.

In Skagway, he built an empire on the same principles as the soap scam—show them just enough to make them believe and think the game was fair. And because of those principles, he never needed to take from others, they were always willing to give.

But, as we've already learned, eventually it all caught up to him in 1898. And when it all came to a head and he was gunned down on the streets of Skagway, there were no more illusions as to the kind of man he was. He was slick, slimy, and slippery. He was Soapy Smith.

Why is it called Smuggler's Cove?

Southeast Alaska's coastline is a rugged mosaic of inlets and hidden bays, each with its own story. But the one we're talking about here, Smuggler's Cove, is known not just for its beauty but for the murmurs of mystery that surround it.

As you know, in the late 19th century, the fevered dreams of the Klondike Gold Rush had cast a spell, drawing thousands to the treacherous trails leading north. And Skagway, once a quiet Tlingit fishing camp, burgeoned into a booming frontier town with its streets teeming with hopeful prospectors, opportunistic merchants, and those who thrived in the shadows.

Just a short trek from the town's clamor, Smuggler's Cove offered a secluded refuge. Its very name hinting at secretive activity, but the name's origins are a little foggy. Some say Lieutenant Commander Nichols of the U.S. Navy gave the Cove the name during an 1883 survey mission. But others suspect the name was earned honestly, whispered only by those who knew its secrets firsthand.

One tale speaks of weary prospectors, disillusioned by the brutal climb up the Chilkoot and the even more brutal odds of striking gold, who turned to more nefarious means of fortune. These men, familiar with every twist and turn of the coastal waterways, found the Cove's sheltered embrace ideal for offloading goods away from the prying eyes of United States Customs Agents. Rumors suggest that under the cover of darkness, shipments of moonshine, furs, and opium, found their way to the eager hands in Skagway, skipping taxes and avoiding questions.

Which brings us to the legend of the *Phantom Sloop*. Locals still speak of this ghostly vessel that appears on foggy nights, gliding silently into the Cove. Some claim it is the spirit of a ship lost to the tides, forever seeking safe harbor. Others say it is no ghost at all, but a clever trick still used by smugglers—lanterns hung from rigged sails to throw off patrol boats while the real cargo comes in quietly by rowboat.

And then there's Soapy.

Soapy Smith, as you know, wasn't just a con man; he was Skagway's kingpin during the gold rush years, and if the stories are true, he didn't limit his influence to the saloons downtown. With a silver tongue and a pistol at his side, Soapy ran gambling halls, crooked telegraph offices, and a protection racket so bold it operated in broad daylight.

But at night? That was a different kind of business.

It's whispered that Soapy, ever the strategist, eyed Smuggler's Cove as the perfect backdoor. The Cove's seclusion made it ideal for off-the-books dealings—whether it was unloading crates of bootleg liquor, arranging discreet meetings with his inner circle, or hiding valuables "confiscated" from his victims. Some say you could see lanterns bobbing on the black water late at night as Soapy's men rowed ashore with parcels wrapped in canvas and surnames they never used twice.

Other tales tell of Soapy retreating to the Cove himself when the heat got too high, pacing the pebbled beach and plotting his next move, always a step ahead until the very end. And as the story goes, when he was gunned down, he had just come back from the Cove, where he'd stashed something no one has ever found.

Of course, these are just stories. Ask

around, and everyone's got a slightly different version.

Today, the trail to Smuggler's Cove is nothing but a favorite hike among locals. It winds through spruce and cedar, crosses a sturdy little bridge, and ends at a quiet stretch of shoreline. Eagles circle above, and if you're lucky, you might spot seals bobbing just offshore. But the Cove still feels like it's watching. Like it remembers.

And if you sit still long enough, you might just hear something strange—the soft clink of glass, the scrape of an oar, the faint snap of a match in the dark. Or maybe it's just the wind playing tricks, the way it always has in places that know how to keep a secret.

And Smuggler's Cove? Well, she's kept plenty.

What are decency laws and the sin tax?

For centuries, whether by church or by state, people have tried to keep solicitation separate from everyday life. And despite its unruly reputation, Skagway was no exception during the Klondike Gold Rush. Not that the oldest profession was ever illegal. After all, that would've been bad for business.

Instead, it was tolerated—a necessary evil, a byproduct of too many men and too much liquor. But the town couldn't just let it go unchecked. The good people of Skagway couldn't have their little frontier settlement turned into another Sodom and Gomorrah. So, the local law enforcement did what it could. They imposed what were called "Decency Laws."

On paper, the rules were simple. A woman must be fully covered whenever visible in public—modesty, enforced by city ordinance.

Sounds easy enough to enforce, right? Wrong. The working girls had a work around. They took to wearing red bloomers and striped stockings under their skirts—loud, unmistakable, and just revealing enough to grab the attention of their clientele. All it took was a well-timed lift when stepping over a puddle, and suddenly, they were advertising plenty.

Clearly, the Decency Laws failed spectacularly.

So, Skagway's moral enforcers tried again. This time, they introduced quarterly court appearances. Every three

months, every known lady of the night
was rounded up, arrested, and taken
before the judge. While there, they were
expected to plead guilty to the charges
and pay a fine. The penalty, $25.

And just like that, they were free to
go back to work.

It was a system that barely pretended
to be anything other than what it was,
a licensing fee. A Sin Tax. Every three
months, the women paid up, the town
turned a blind eye, and business carried
on as usual. And this Sin Tax paid for
all sorts of things. For instance, it kept
the streetlamps burning, the roads
maintained, and—most notably—funded
the very law enforcement that kept
bringing these girls in.

Yes. That's right. The women who
were fined into submission were also the
ones who were, quite literally, keeping
Skagway's lights on. Go figure. And
for a while, nobody questioned it. The
arrangement was understood, if not

exactly fair. But then, in 1952, two women decided they weren't going to play along.

Their names were Rose Arnold and Ruth Brown—two working women who ran a lucrative crib near the army barracks. And on a cold January in Skagway, they became the first to plead not guilty to the chargers.

And for a moment, it almost worked. Rose managed to avoid anything worse than a minor conviction. But Ruth, on the other hand, was not so lucky. As the crib's business owner, she was targeted. The court acquitted her once but then she was re-arrested. And again. And again. See, the system wasn't built to let women like her win, and by the time they were finished with her, she was forced to pay not only the $25 fine, but an additional $141 in court fees—which, to put this into perspective, roughly equates to $5,000 today.

Needless to say, Rose and Ruth packed up shop and left town. But they didn't go back south. They didn't slink away in defeat. Instead, they left Skagway behind and headed to Juneau, where they changed their names and slipped beyond the reach of official records.

Maybe they started over. Maybe they found a place where the system didn't take as much as it gave. No one will ever know.

As for Skagway, it continued to keep its lamps lit and its streets patched, but it never figured out how to reconcile the paradox it was built on—how vice and virtue had to tango together to keep the town alive. It is the kind of paradox that lingers in the bones of a town, waiting for someone to come along and ask who really paid the price for progress.

And more often than not, the answer is the same. The women. The ones the world let slip through its cracks when it asked more than they could give.

Paradise?
In an alley in Skagway?
Really?

At first glance, you'd be forgiven for walking right past it. Paradise Alley, as it's called, isn't much to look at these days—a couple of parked cars, a battered garbage can, and the ever-present scent of fryer grease wafting from the inn next door. But names in Skagway have a habit of carrying more weight than they let on.

And if you've read the previous tale referencing the good-time girls, you might already be leaning in, wondering how this unremarkable stretch of town ended up with such a contradictory name.

In 1898, this alley was alive with an altogether different kind of energy. Lined with wooden cribs—shack-like structures that were both practical and painfully public—it was the domain of the working women who made their livings on the street. They weathered the north in a way that very few could, carving out what existence was possible in a town that was far better at forgetting than forgiving.

In a single crib as many as four women might work, each staking her claim to a bed and little else. And privacy came in the form of thin sheets draped between corners which tended to flutter in the wind—among other things.

But even in Skagway's underworld, there was a hierarchy. At the top were the brothel girls, working under the watchful eye of a madam. Their meals provided and their quarters—at least compared to other girls—were secure. And for fifteen

minutes of their time, one would have to
fork over five dollars—a small fortune in
those days.

Beneath them were the crib girls,
independent in name only. Most of
these women worked under a pimp who
provided neither safety nor sustenance.
Their going rate for that same fifteen
minutes? Three dollars.

And at the very bottom were the
streetwalkers, the ones with nowhere
to go but the alleyways like the one we
are discussing in this story. Alone and
exposed, their fee was a single dollar for
fifteen minutes of their time—less a price
than a reflection of the dire conditions of
their reality.

It was a grim economy, but in
Paradise Alley, it was a predictable one.
No matter your budget, Skagway could
provide.

But let's pause here. It would be easy
to leave this as a tale of resilience, a nod
to the adaptability of those who lived on

society's fringes. But behind grinning brothel doors, the crib sheets waving in the wind, and the cash changing hands, there were darker truths—ones not spoken of often in the daylight.

At the height of the Klondike Gold Rush, there were some 300 working women in Skagway. Some arrived chasing dreams of something better, only to find themselves out of options and out of time. For others, the oldest profession was a calculated choice—a way to scrape together enough money to leave, to start over somewhere else. And then there were those for whom choice had never been part of the equation at all.

That's the part of history that towns don't put on their plaques.

But Skagway, in all its contradictions, has never been a place that fits neatly into the chapters of history. The same streets that once bustled with fortune seekers and card sharks, con men and dreamers, were also walked by those just trying to make it to another sunrise. Some of them made it. Some of them did not.

Today though, locals are happy to celebrate that Skagway is a different place. Over half its locally owned businesses are run by women—fierce, tenacious women who carry forward the legacy of their predecessors.

But if you step into Paradise Alley, past the cars and the peeling paint, you might just gain a deeper appreciation for those who came before—who worked, who fought to survive, and who, against all odds, left their mark on this little Alaskan town.

What kind of work —other than the obvious— was available for women during the gold rush?

I'd like to take a second to point out that, although it did happen, women did not always simply slip through the cracks in Southeast Alaska. Many came up to Alaska and led long and lucrative lives up north.

But it's at about this point that I'm guessing you're thinking that all there was for women was the industry. And I don't blame you for that. Up until this point,

I've made it abundantly clear that there was no shortage of "entertainment" in Skagway in the late 1800s. Those miners were never left wanting. But the answer is, of course, no. Some worked in kitchens or ran the inns. Others owned shops or managed storefronts. But in Skagway, the lucky ones, well, they were either performers or percentage girls. And if you don't know what a percentage girl is—just keep reading.

So, picture this, you step into a Skagway saloon during the gold rush. The room is thick with pipe smoke and whiskey breath. The music's loud, the air is warm, and the floor is alive with twirling skirts. Those women? They were the percentage girls.

For a dollar, they'd dance with you for a song for which they'd make a fifty percent commission. You get thirsty? Well, they get a piece of that, too. Twenty-five percent of any drinks bought for them or in their presence went right into their pocket.

And getting these drinks bought for them wasn't hard. After a dance or two, any half-inebriated miner could be convinced his partner needed a little refreshment. The real trick, though, is staying sober. Thankfully, they had a plan for that.

The girls had a system. They'd waltz up to the bar, order a whiskey, and flash the bartender a wink. This was the signal. And once received, the bartender would—instead of liquor—pour watered-down iced tea into a shot glass and charge top-shelf prices. That way, the girls kept their wits about them while not sacrificing profits.

It was good money, and many a lady applied for these positions, but it didn't compare to what the performers made. The entertainers pulled in $150 a week, which didn't include their own twenty-five percent drink commissions. Not to mention, they could keep anything else that they could convince a man to part with. And no one played the game better than Cad Wilson.

According to the locals, Cad arrived in Skagway in 1898. And from news reports, we can deduce that she wasn't known for being particularly beautiful, nor did she have any discernible talent. But that didn't stop her from becoming the highest-paid performer on the Pacific Coast.

Her act was suggestive—not by today's standards, but by those of the time. It was profoundly provocative. On some nights, she'd step up onto the stage, her eyes slow and deliberate, her hands trailing down to the hem of her skirt. And then, in a move that thrilled her enthusiastic male fans, she'd lift the skirt just high enough to reveal her ankles.

Now, some of you might be a little disappointed to hear that, but back then that's all it took.

Men, thrilled beyond reason at the sight of her boot-clad ankle, would dig into their pockets and hurl their gold and silver dollars at her feet. But Cad didn't just stand there and take it. No. Instead, she'd give them somewhere to aim.

As the gold came—literally—flying in, Cad got a good firm grip on her skirt with both hands and tried to catch the little nuggets with her skirt.

Well, after a while, the fabric would get heavy. And when it became too much to hold, she'd bend down, grasp the hem a little higher, and give the men a little more to work for. The more they threw, the more she lifted until, eventually, she was giving everyone a gander at her undergarments. It was a foolproof gimmick.

But that wasn't Cad's only trick. Cad also offered private performances. And from what I've been told, on at least one occasion, a man paid her $75,000 for a single night.

Now, before you assume the obvious, no. She did not sleep with him.

The man just wanted to watch her bathe … in champagne.

At the time, a bottle of champagne in Skagway ran about $30. And Cad, being the entrepreneur that she was, still made twenty-five percent commission on drinks. So, when the offer came in, of course, she accepted. And as she ascended the stairs, she'd turn to tease the man with the promise of a spectacle. But just as she reached the landing, she turned and gave him a regretful smile and told him that she just wasn't the kind of woman to allow a man to watch her bathe.

The man wasn't pleased, but Cad had a way about her. She convinced him to descend the stairs, belly up to the bar, and have a drink on her tab, and imagine her doing it.

And what choice did he have? None.

So, down he went, and up she went, and a bath was had. But Cad only being a somewhat honest woman, didn't let all that good liquor go to waste. And when she was finished, she rebottled it all and sold it right back to the bar! Cad made double that night, and cemented her legacy in Skagway's folklore.

Now, not everyone had Cad's cunning, but during the gold rush, the best of them found ways to turn the game in their favor. They danced, they drank or pretended to, and they carved out lives in a town that didn't offer much mercy. Some, like Cad, managed to leave with their pockets full.

How many ghosts live in Ghost Alley?

So, if you've been following along with the *Northern Narratives Series*, you've probably noticed a few recurring themes. Sure, there's plenty of gold, gold seekers, and gold mining, but that's not what I'm talking about here. No, the common thread I'm talking about is ghosts. And for those of you waiting for the next haunt, your patience has finally paid off.

Skagway is no stranger to the undead. Just ask around, and you'll hear stories of spirits lurking in just about every building in town. But one place in particular deserves its spot in these pages, not just because it's haunted, but because it's a local favorite. They call it Ghost Alley.

Now, this is not its official name, but it's what people say when they talk about the narrow passage off Broadway, shadowed by the remains of one specific run-down building. Nature has mostly taken it back—trees pressing in, vines creeping over the frame—but during the gold rush, this structure was the servant quarters of the Poland House Hotel. It was home to the butler, his wife, and their teenage daughter. As ghost stories typically go, things didn't exactly end well for these three.

And in this story, things took a turn for the worse when the daughter became pregnant; scandal enough in a town like Skagway where virtue was in short supply but hypocrisy never was. Even worse, the young women shared her desire to have the child despite the difficulties of being a single mother at this time.

Unfortunately, fate had other plans. The baby was stillborn. And rather than risk additional unwanted attention, her parents buried the infant in an unmarked grave in the woods. They thought that would be the end of it. It wasn't.

Grief consumed the would-be mother. She wouldn't eat. She wouldn't sleep. And then, one night, she swore she heard her baby crying for her in the woods. Before her parents could stop her, she ran into the freezing dark, barefoot and delirious, with nothing on but her nightdress. She survived but, after this incident, her parents knew they couldn't handle her any longer. So, she was sent down south to Seattle with her mother, where she was placed in an asylum. As for her father, he stayed behind, working and pretending things could go back to normal.

But from what I've been told, the baby's cries didn't stop.

At first, he thought someone in town was mocking him, taking pleasure in his family's misfortune. So, he did what any man in his position would do, he grabbed his shotgun and went looking. But there was no one to be found.

The sound continued, night after night and, eventually, the sleeplessness wore him down. His temper turned sharp and his paranoia got worse which led to him accusing friends and strangers alike. That is, until, one night, a single gunshot rang out, and by morning, the town knew he had ended the crying himself.

But from what I hear, even now, especially in the deep quiet of winter when the snow is falling softly, folks say they still see smoke curling up from the old chimney, they hear a baby's cry, and the crackle of a single gunshot. And if you get too close to the ruins, some even claim that you might just meet the spirit of that crazed man—angry and accusing you of trying to trick him.

The butler is not the friendliest spirit in Skagway, and he's not the only one either. See, as Skagway's reputation grew, it started drawing attention—not just from prospectors, but from people who weren't thrilled about what was happening here. And if you're wondering which doom-laden prophecy preacher still lingers around these parts, well, you'll just have to keep reading.

Who is Mabel Ouray?

By now, you know the story. In 1898, Skagway was drowning in a sea of desperate men, rushing to its shores in search of gold. But while prospectors came north for fortune, others came looking for something else—lost souls. Among them was Mabel Ouray.

Mabel was a missionary, but she wasn't content with just preaching in a pulpit. She had a habit of taking her sermons straight to the source—brothels, crib rooms, anywhere a woman was making a living the old-fashioned way.

She'd stand outside and deliver fire-and-brimstone at full volume, warning of eternal damnation and the wages of sin.

Needless to say, she wasn't great for business. So, the working women of Skagway did what they had to do. When they saw Mabel coming down the street, they'd slip her a few dollars to take her sermon elsewhere. And Mabel, never one to turn down a donation, would accept the cash and move along to the next brothel and repeat the process. As it turns out, even the righteous could make a decent living in a den of sin.

But here's the thing—Mabel wasn't pocketing the money. No. She was saving it. She put every single dollar towards her project, Skagway's very own Peniel Mission House.

The mission wasn't just a shelter for women, it was a lifeline. It offered food, clothing, job training, and even medical care for women who wanted out. And Mabel, ever the realist, didn't stop there.

She had a knack for matchmaking and arranged marriages for many of these women in the Lower Forty-Eight. And if it worked out, Mabel would even personally pay for their passage south.

The women knew where the money was going. They knew that, while paying Mabel kept their business booming, they were also investing in their own futures. For should they fall on hard times, Mabel and the mission would be there for them.

Now, her methods were unorthodox. But in a town where people saw many of these women as disposable, Mabel was one of the people standing up for these working girls.

Today, the old Mission House still stands, though it is now owned by the National Park Service and is used for seasonal employee housing. But, as the story goes, the place hasn't entirely let go of its past.

Some of Mabel's original furniture is still in the building—paintings, chairs, and a few things that shouldn't have survived this long. And if you move them, they don't stay moved. More than one worker has woken up to find Mabel's Bible sitting on their bedside table. Paintings have reappeared on walls even after being tossed in the trash. Other workers have even sworn they've heard distant preaching outside their window in the dead of night. And lastly, workers have found out that cash never stays in the house for long. It just disappears.

Now, whether you believe in ghosts or just think the seasoned workers enjoy messing with the newcomers doesn't really matter. Because regardless of what you believe, Mabel's mark isn't just etched onto that building—its seared into Skagway's history. And for all of the men who passed through town chasing their riches, she was the one who actually built something that lasted.

What is the story behind the explosion on the *Clara Nevada?*

They say the *Clara Nevada* went down fast—too fast for anyone to survive, too fast for anyone to know exactly what happened. But stories, like smoke, have a way of lingering.

It was the heart of winter, 1898, and gold rush fever was burning hotter than ever. Prospectors were pouring into Skagway, weighed down by dreams and dynamite. And the *Clara Nevada*, a once-proud steamship that had been refitted for passenger service, was docked and ready.

She'd been a government survey ship once, but now she was packed with men desperate to get south with gold—some say hidden in false-bottom trunks or sewn into the hems of coats.

She left Skagway bound for Seattle by way of Lynn Canal. And according to the manifest, there were roughly 40 passengers and crew on board. But some manifest lists back then were sketchy, with men buying last-minute tickets with aliases used to dodge debts. It was a different time.

What we do know is that she didn't make it far. Just before midnight, a flash lit up the cold February sky, followed by a sound so loud it echoed all the way back to Skagway. Then a fire broke out on board. Some say the *Clara Nevada* struck a submerged rock and the impact ignited her cargo. Others whisper of dynamite stowed illegally below deck. Unfortunately, the truth went down with the ship.

Only one body was ever found washed ashore with a watch still ticking, and a pair of boots so new the soles hadn't scuffed. Everything else—passengers, crew, ship, and rumored gold—vanished beneath the waves.

And that's when the stories really started.

One story goes like this: there was no explosion, no accident. The whole thing was a setup. A small group of crewmen, led by the captain himself, hatched a plan to fake the ship's destruction and make off with the gold. They offloaded the treasure before departure, and set the ship on fire to burn in open water. And then they disappeared into the dark.

Another tale tells of a rival shipping company—cutthroat competitors who sabotaged the *Clara Nevada* to scare passengers into buying tickets elsewhere. According to this version, the fire was deliberate and the ship was a casualty of a shadow war on Southeast Alaska's waters.

And then there's the romantic version, the one that claims a stowaway lit the fire—either a jealous lover or a man avenging his brother lost on a previous voyage. No gold, no conspiracy—just grief and flames.

Either way, regardless of how she sank, the *Clara Nevada* now resides in her final resting place just off of Eldred Rock, 30 feet below the surface guarded by cold currents.

Divers have visited the wreckage over the years. They've brought up pieces of metal, an occasional plate, or a shoe buckle. But no gold, no manifest, and no clear answers.

But what makes the *Clara Nevada* more than just another shipwreck isn't the gold, it's the fact that the stories haven't stopped—stories which have captured the imaginations of locals and tourists alike.

Today, the Eldred Rock Lighthouse stands above the wreckage watching over this lonely stretch of water that has claimed more than one soul. It doesn't blink nor speak, but sometimes you get the sense that the lighthouse knows more than it is letting on.

And if you walk the beaches in that part of Lynn Canal, especially after a storm, you might still find a piece of the *Clara Nevada*—a twisted bolt, a scorched plank, the kind of thing that feels older than it ought to be.

Pick it up if you want, some say the gold's still out there. Just be warned, so are the ghosts.

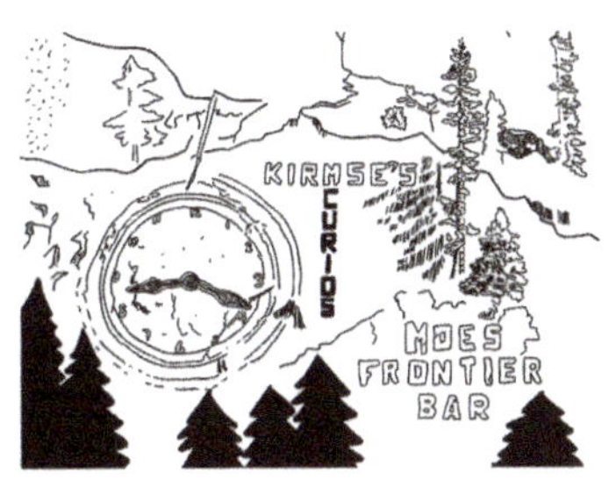

How does one get their advertisement on a mountain?

If you've traveled to Skagway, you've seen them. No way around it. They are quite literally painted on the rock face above town. They are, of course, not the only oddity in Skagway, not by a long shot, but they are the most noticeable. And if you ask around, you'll hear that some of these advertisements have been around since the Klondike Gold Rush.

But why would a town allow its businesses to slap their name across the mountain like graffiti with a business license. Every local has a different version of the story, and most of them sound just convincing enough to be true.

The general agreement goes something like this, at the height of the gold rush, businesses needed to advertise. But the docks back then weren't where they are today. Skagway's waterfront has been stretched outward, eating into the inlet with layers of gravel and time. And in those early days, the docks sat further inland, meaning ships full of prospectors had an unbroken view of the hills as they approached. A perfect, unavoidable billboard.

At first, the shops did it the normal way by erecting wooden signs promising warm beds, hot meals, and honest deals! But Skagway is home to the north wind, and that wind isn't kind to anything that stands too long. The wind comes down the channel like a hammer flattening anything not bolted to the bedrock. Billboards, no matter how well built they were, simply didn't last long.

There's an old saying in town, you can either do things the right way, do things the wrong way, or you can do things the Skagway. And that's exactly what they did. If the wind wanted to take down their signs, the people of town would make one the wind couldn't take.

So, Skagway did what Skagway does and folks began climbing the mountain and painting their messages straight onto the rock. No regulations, no lumber required. And once something is painted onto Skagway's mountain, well, good luck getting rid of it.

That's why, even now, when one looks up at the mountain that towers over town, they'll see those old advertisements clinging to the cliffs since the gold rush, some larger than even the buildings they once represented. Most people wouldn't call it history. Most people wouldn't call it art. But in Skagway, it's a little bit of both.

Of all of the places,
why build a road to Skagway?

Alaska has no shortage of ways to remind you that it isn't like anywhere else in this world. There's wilderness and untouched landscapes, raw and unrepentant. The midnight sun, which stretches the day, sometimes to its breaking point. Not to mention glaciers, northern lights, and the sort of wildlife that looks at you like you're the one trespassing. This list is long, b ut the aspect of Alaska I want to focus on in this story is its remoteness.

Now, seclusion isn't exclusive to

Alaska. There are plenty of places just as cut off, some even more so. Pockets of Canada's far north, for example, or Siberia. These are places that you're likely not going to find yourself unless you had to. But what sets Alaska apart isn't just its isolation, it is its commitment to connectivity. And in some places, our state is willing to move mountains—sometimes literally—to make it happen.

Which begs the question, why, in all of Alaska's roadless expanse, did the state decide to build a highway leading to Skagway, a town of 800 people, when its own capital—Juneau—has no road in or out? And to answer that question, we must search somewhere between geography and history.

First, let's observe the land itself. What separates Southeast Alaska from Canada is the Juneau Icefield, a vast stretch of glaciers and mountain ranges that are as impassable as they are indifferent to human ambition. The shortest, least impossible route across is located just outside of Skagway. So, if there was ever going to be a road connecting this region to the rest of the world, this was the only logical choice.

But according to the locals, the real reason Skagway got its road wasn't just about topography. No. It was about war.

And to get to the heart of the matter, we are going to have to travel back to December 7, 1941, to Pearl Harbor. The United States, until then sitting on the sidelines of World War II, suddenly found itself dragged into the fray. What followed was a series of intense campaigns—Guadalcanal, Iwo Jima, Okinawa—battles you've likely heard about, battles that shaped history. But what you probably haven't heard about is what was happening in Alaska at this very same time.

That's right, while American forces were pushing west, the Japanese were also pushing east. All the way to Alaska.

The invasion of the Aleutian Islands—Attu and Kiska—meant that, for the first time since the War of 1812, foreign troops occupied American soil. And that meant Alaska was no longer just a frontier anymore, it was a battleground.

The problem was logistics. Getting troops and supplies to the Aleutians by ship meant traveling large stretches of open ocean, leaving them vulnerable to enemies and unpredictable weather. So, the allies needed another way.

The solution? Overland through Canada. The problem? A road didn't exist.

So, with wartime necessity trumping all else, the United States and Canada threw their armies into the wilderness to build one. And in just seven months, they carved a road through some of the roughest terrain on the continent, creating a crucial overland route for military transport. The Alaskan-Canadian Military Highway, now known as the Alaska Highway or Alcan, was born.

But there was still the matter of the last stretch—getting the road system to the Pacific Ocean.

This is where Skagway comes in. The White Pass had already made its mark on history as a gold rush gateway, but now it would assume a new role. The pass offered the only viable break in the icefield, and the only way to move equipment and personnel out to the coast. But making it passable for military convoys meant blasting through rock, cutting into permafrost, and building a road that had no business existing.

But, where there's a will—and enough dynamite—there's a way. And once the road was complete, Skagway became a crucial supply link in a war thousands of miles away.

And yet, for all its significance, this piece of history is rarely told outside of Southeast Alaska. Tourists coming through today mostly opt for the train, latching onto its gold rush legacy rather than the war-era pavement running beside it.

Now, I'm not knocking the train—it's an incredible experience. And without it, the Klondike Gold Rush might not have been what it was. But if this story leaves you with anything, it's this; that short 30-mile stretch of highway, one barely anyone thinks twice about, might have changed the outcome of World War II. And without it, all us Alaskans might have ended up speaking a very different language.

Author's note

As you come to the end of this book of tall tales, we hope you have enjoyed the wild adventures and colorful characters that have been brought to life through the histories, stories, and folklore that have shaped Alaska and the people who call her home.

But it is important to remember that, although these tales have been shared and passed down by locals over the years, they are not entirely factual. They are the stuff of legend and imagination, embellished with each retelling to become bigger and more outrageous than before.

Nonetheless, these stories have become an integral part of the fabric of Alaska's history and culture, and they continue to inspire and entertain new generations of storytellers and listeners.

So, as you put down this book, remember to take these tales with a grain of salt, and to appreciate them for what they are: a testament to the enduring spirit of the Last Frontier, and to the power of a good story to captivate and delight us all.

Who's your author?

The author telling these tall tales wasn't born and raised in Alaska, but he'll tell you he's from Alaska. He'll tell you that because he's spent the last eight years of his life living in Juneau. But it wasn't the picturesque landscapes that brought him here though. No. Instead, it was an unexpected encounter in the heart of South America that made his life take this remarkable turn.

That's right, he followed a woman all the way up north, past the sixtieth parallel.

However, their initial meeting was bittersweet. Their whirlwind romance in South America only lasted three weeks because she had a job to get back to in Alaska and, at the time, he had a company to run back home. So, they said farewell and went their separate ways.

But, upon getting home, our author knew that something was different.

Something about that girl had left an undeniable mark on his heart. And, driven by this unshakable feeling, he planned a trip to visit her in Juneau.

From the moment he landed in Alaska, he was struck by the towering mountains, lush forests, and the pristine waters reflecting the azure sky above. But, if you ask him now, it was the simple moments spent with the woman he loved that left the deepest impression. Whether it was sharing stories over a crackling fire or embarking on an impromptu hike up Blueberry Hill, every moment felt like a cherished memory.

And with each passing moment they spent together, the author's resolve to build a future with her grew stronger. So, upon returning home, with unwavering determination, he sold his shares in the company and everything else he owned, and embarked on the greatest adventure of his life.

Eight years later, he's now married to the woman he met in South America, and a proud resident of Juneau. A place that has both become his home and the backdrop to his love story—the greatest story he'll ever tell.

So, if you're in Juneau, go ahead and make your way on down to the Red Dog Saloon. And if you're lucky, you might just find him there signing books and passing out pints from behind the bar—or, more likely, drinking them on the other side.